Gwen

The Alien Bride

Editorial Director: Marge Kennedy
Retold by John W. Kennedy
Based on Ben 10 Episode #46:
Big Fat Alien Wedding by Eugene Son

little monks on the wisdom tree

Dear Diary,

I'm on my way to a family wedding in Texas with my Grandpa Max and geeky superhero cousin, Ben.

Ben and I are both in the wedding party. I'm the flower girl, and he's the ring bearer. I'm happy and he's not - exactly as it should be!

But then Ben hasn't been a happy camper since I discovered my magical powers while fighting the evil sorcerer Hex and his not-so-nice niece Charmcaster.

But that's his problem. I'm just looking forward to a beautiful wedding - and a break from fighting super villains from all over the galaxy.

You know it's a Tennyson family event when you're hoping that no invasions from outer space ruin the day!

Gwen

Table of Contents

CHAPTER 1:
A Big Fat Texas Wedding

Struggling for air, 10-year-old Ben Tennyson reached for his watch-like Omnitrix and gasped, "Must…go…hero."

But before Ben could activate the device that linked his DNA to that of superheroes from throughout the universe, a large hand reached out to stop him. Ben struggled, but it was useless. He was no match for his opponent.

"You better loosen that bow tie," his same-age cousin, Gwen, chimed in. "Ben's brain needs all the oxygen it can get."

"I know," responded Grandpa Max as he relaxed the knot that held Ben's tie around his neck. "Boy," he added, "what a baby! It's not that tight."

"The only thing worse than going to a stupid, old, boring wedding," Ben griped while dramatically gulping oxygen, "is being in one – and being forced to wear a lame-o tuxedo! Why can't they find another ring bearer?!"

“It’s only for one day,” Grandpa Max huffed. “You’ll live!”

“I’m looking forward to the wedding,” Gwen beamed. “I’ve never been a flower girl before.”

“Lucky you!” Ben sarcastically replied.

“Okay, the tuxedo fits,” Grandpa Max decreed. “You can take it off – for now.” With that, Ben eagerly changed back into his regular clothes.

A short time later, the Tennysons arrived at the Grand Revelle Hotel, the large ranch-style hotel about 40 miles outside of Dallas. Upon exiting the Rustbucket, Grandpa Max’s old Recreational Vehicle (RV), they were warmly greeted by Grandpa Max’s nephew, Joel, and his bride-to-be, Camille.

“Uncle Max!” Joel called out. “I’m so glad you’re here!”

“Joel!” Grandpa Max smiled, while embracing him in a big bear hug. Then, turning toward Camille, Grandpa Max added, “And this must be your beautiful bride!”

"It's so nice to meet you," Camille responded. "Joel has told me so much about you."

"Good things, I hope," Grandpa Max laughed.

"Very good," Camille assured him with a smile.

"Uncle Max," Joel said. "I need to talk with you. I'm hoping you can talk some sense into my parents."

"Why? What's the problem?" Grandpa Max asked.

But before Joel could answer…

"MAX!" thundered a voice from behind.

They all turned around as Big Gordon Tennyson – a spitting image of Grandpa Max (if Grandpa Max were a bit thinner, had a mustache, and wore a big black cowboy hat) – and his wife walked toward them.

"Betty Jean! Gordon!" Grandpa Max exclaimed. "It's been so long," he said. "I bet you don't even recognize my grandkids, Gwen and Ben!"

Gwen and Ben extended their hands to their aunt and uncle, but Big Gordon clearly had something besides greetings on his mind.

"Max," he said, "we're so glad you're here. Maybe you can talk some sense into these kids."

"What do you mean?" Grandpa Max replied.

"This whole wedding is a terrible mistake!" Big Gordon insisted.

"This whole wedding is a terrible mistake?" Grandpa Max repeated incredulously.

"See?" Gordon said to Joel. "Listen to your Uncle Max."

"Now, Gordon," came another voice. "The kids are grown-ups. Who are we to get in their way?"

The group turned toward the voice and saw a couple approach from the hotel's main entrance.

"Meet my parents, Mr. and Mrs. Mann," Camille said, as she introduced her mom and dad to each of her soon-to-be in-laws.

"I'm sorry we had to meet under such awkward circumstances," Mrs. Mann apologized, as she shook Grandpa Max's hand.

"So are we!" Big Gordon and Betty Jean announced in unison.

With that, the rather-not-be future in-laws engaged in a fierce staredown that ended only when both sides turned and headed in opposite directions.

"Maybe this wedding won't be so boring after all," an amused Ben whispered to the silently giggling Gwen. But Grandpa Max looked sympathetically at Joel and Camille and said, "Don't worry. It's all gonna work out."

Attempting to change the subject, Gwen cleared her throat and asked, "So, as flower girl, what exactly are my official duties?"

"Oh, Gwen, I'm sorry," Joel replied. "Someone should have told you. Camille's little cousin Lucy was able to make it after all. But thanks for being willing to pinch-hit for her."

"Sure," responded Gwen, trying to mask her disappointment. "Think nothing of it."

"Oh, please tell me you got another ring bearer, too," Ben pleaded hopefully.

“Oh, nothing changes for you,” Joel answered, “except that you’ll be dancing with Lucy at the reception.”

“D-Dancing?!” Ben stammered. “I don’t know how to dance!”

“I guess you’d better learn,” Joel teased, adding with a wink, “you don’t wanna look like a mega-dweeb out there on the dance floor.”

“You’ll be fine,” Camille reassured him as she and Joel headed toward the hotel’s lobby.

“This wedding,” Ben noted, “went from being boring to maybe funny to becoming a nightmare in about a minute.”

“Tell me about it,” replied Gwen, no longer hiding her annoyance over losing the flower-girl gig.

But neither of them could know just how bad things were about to get.

CHAPTER 2:
Alien Wedding Crasher

That night, Gwen, Ben, and Grandpa Max retired to their hotel suite. With Grandpa Max and Ben snoring in stereo, Gwen decided to get dressed and head out onto the balcony to enjoy the clear night sky. But, when she stepped outside, the night was anything but clear. A gray haze covered the landscape – and she smelled smoke!

When she looked down at the grounds that surrounded the hotel, she gasped as she saw flames engulfing several of the outside structures, including one of the gazebos!

"FIRE!" Gwen screamed. Grandpa Max and Ben awoke and immediately ran onto the terrace, as lights from all over the hotel lit up.

"Goin' hero – this time for real!" Ben proclaimed, as he pressed his Omnitrix and became...CANNONBOLT!

The black, white, and yellow Neburian Pelarota curled his chubby body into a ball and hurled himself downward toward the hotel's large man-made lake.

“CANNONBOLT CANNONBALL!” Ben shouted gleefully, as he splashed into the pond, creating watery waves that drenched and extinguished the scattered flames.

The hotel was now safe, and Ben, as Cannonbolt, was feeling pretty good as he sloshed toward the edge of the water. But, instead of being greeted as a hero, he found himself staring into the barrels of two futuristic laser rifles!

“Boy, the lifeguards around here are really strict!” he exclaimed before realizing that the high-tech weaponry was being held by Big Gordon and Betty Jean.

“A Neburian Pelarota!” Big Gordon hollered as if he had just bagged the catch of a lifetime.

“It’s an alien wedding crasher!” declared Betty Jean. “Who sent you?!” she demanded.

“Nobody!” Cannonbolt earnestly replied. “I don’t even wanna be here!”

Big Gordon lowered his rifle, but Betty Jean kept hers steadily aimed at the alien.

“Don’t move,” she warned.

Cannonbolt was relieved to see help show up.

"What's going on?!" Joel called out as he, Grandpa Max, and Gwen arrived on the scene.

"This alien is trying to ruin the wedding," Betty Jean asserted as she lowered her rifle, much to Cannonbolt's relief.

"I was trying to save the wedding!" Cannonbolt insisted.

"I think he's telling the truth," Grandpa Max said.

"We'd better not take any chances," Betty Jean countered. "You know that we can't trust aliens."

Betty Jean raised her laser rifle again and was about to fire, when Gwen whispered the magic words *Camouphlat Vaporis!*

Suddenly, her hand glowed with a blue aura, and the water from the lake emitted huge puffs of blinding white steam that gave Cannonbolt the opportunity to leap out of the lake.

"He's getting away!" Big Gordon shouted. He and his wife then began blasting away at everything in sight!

As the steam lifted, Joel and Grandpa Max grabbed the laser rifles from Big Gordon and Betty Jean.

"Put these things away!" Joel shouted. "This is a hotel, not a shooting range!"

"But that – thing – is still out there," Big Gordon argued.

"I don't care!" Joel shouted. "Just promise me that you won't take out any weapons for the rest of the weekend!"

Meanwhile, Cannonbolt had rolled into the wooded area at the edge of the hotel grounds.

"That was close," he muttered to himself. "Now, where am I?" he wondered as he scratched his head and looked around.

But before he could get his bearings, a puddle of mud began taking on a strange alien shape behind him. Cannonbolt turned around just as the muddy monster was reaching out to engulf him.

Cannonbolt again rolled into a ball and gyrated away just as the giant sludge beast lunged forward, splattering itself on the ground before reformulating and preparing for another attack!

Cannonbolt, however, wasn't waiting around. He reversed course and threw himself directly at the oozy ogre as both combatants resprouted limbs and engaged in furious paw-to-icky-muck combat. But then the Omnitrix symbol on Cannonbolt's forehead began beeping. He knew he had just seconds to get away before he changed back into Ben!

He intentionally let the amorphous mammoth whack him with his shapeless limb, hurtling him like a muddy baseball toward the fence.

In midair, Cannonbolt transformed back into Ben, who, clad only in his underwear, landed in a cluster of bushes.

The mud monster, its eyes emitting a purple glow, looked directly at him and began approaching. With a twelve-foot-high stone wall behind him, Ben was cornered, and it was too soon to transform into another superhero! He fearfully awaited his fate.

Then he heard a familiar voice.

"Ben, where are you?" Gwen called out from the distance.

The murky miscreant looked over its slimy shoulder. As Gwen approached, it melted into a puddle of mush and oozed back into the ground until it disappeared completely.

As Ben climbed out from behind the bushes, Gwen laughed and called out, "Grandpa Max, the half-naked dweeb is over here!"

"I'm glad you find this amusing," Ben remarked sarcastically.

"Sorry," Gwen apologized with a grin. "Are you okay?"

"Let's just say I hate weddings," Ben replied while nursing a bump on his head.

CHAPTER 3:
Intergalactic Love Story

Later, Gwen, Ben, and Grandpa Max huddled in the Rustbucket, where Grandpa Max applied an ice pack to Ben's bruised forehead.

"I guess I forgot to mention that Gordon and Betty Jean are Plumbers," Grandpa Max confessed.

"You mean those two whack jobs were members of that top-secret alien-fighting organization you belonged to?" Gwen exclaimed in disbelief. "They don't seem like heroes to me."

"Hey, that's my brother and his wife you're talking about!" Grandpa Max replied. "But, yes, those 'whack jobs' were Plumbers."

"The other thing I forgot to mention," Grandpa Max said, "is that the bride and her family are aliens."

"But they don't look like aliens," Ben noted.

"They're just in disguise for the wedding," Grandpa Max explained. "Actually, they're Sludges, shape-shifting aliens that the Plumbers have been at war with for generations.

“A few years ago,” Grandpa Max continued, “Joel met Camille at a party. She, of course, was disguised as a human. By the time she told Joel about her background, it didn’t matter. They were in love. Their relationship has become the basis for a truce between the Plumbers and the Sludges. This will be the first-ever wedding between an Earthling and a Sludge. The hope is that their union will lead to a lasting peace between our worlds.”

“It looks like someone doesn’t want that to happen,” Gwen surmised.

“We’d better all keep our eyes open,” Grandpa Max advised.

The next day, a pre-wedding luncheon was held in the hotel’s banquet hall.

“A toast!” Mr. Mann proclaimed, as he raised his champagne glass. “To two people from two different worlds, may they both live happily ever after.”

Most of the attendees lifted their glasses, smiling at the happy couple.

"Here, here!" seconded Grandpa Max, joining in toasting his nephew and his bride-to-be. The clinking of glasses and the bursts of light from camera flashes added to the festive mood. But conspicuously, Big Gordon and Betty Jean did not participate in the revelry. Instead, they stared coldly ahead at the alien bride, each of them hoping against the hope that the couple embodied.

Meanwhile, over at the kids' table, Gwen and Ben were joined by Camille's blonde 10-year-old cousin, Lucy.

"I'm so excited about being the flower girl," Lucy bragged. "I'm gonna be the cutest girl at the wedding! Everyone will be watching me!" Gwen and Ben looked at each other and rolled their eyes. Then, looking straight at Ben, Lucy said, "We'll be dancing in front of everyone tomorrow! Isn't that great?!"

"Yeah, great!" Ben answered with mock enthusiasm.

As Lucy skipped off happily, Ben dropped his head to the table in dread.

"I want to disappear, not dance," he groaned.

"I should just let you squirm," Gwen remarked, "but I did take cotillion for three years."

Ben gave his cousin a blank stare.

"What's a co-whatever you said?" he asked.

"Oh, never mind," Gwen sighed. "What I'm saying is that I can teach you to dance."

"Yeah," Ben haltingly replied, "I'll think about it – NOT!"

CRASH!

Gwen and Ben looked across the banquet hall, where an angry-looking caterer had just thrown down a stack of china dishes.

"Camille!" the caterer screamed, to everyone's dismay. "I am not letting you marry a filthy human without a fight!" Then, before everyone's eyes, the caterer shape-shifted into a huge purple Sludge!

"That's my ex-boyfriend!" Camille gasped.

"Charming guy," Joel replied dryly.

The giant mud beast then elongated his liquidy limbs and began hurling tables and chairs across the room.

"I'd say now's a good time to 'go hero,'" Gwen suggested.

Taking his cousin's advice, Ben ducked under the table, pressed his Omnitrix and became the emerald giant known as...DIAMONDHEAD!

The scorned Sludge then stretched out his muddy arm and grabbed Joel in his slimy palm!

"If I can't have Camille, then neither can you!" he declared, as he prepared to throw the helpless groom out the window.

"Back off, dirt bag!" Diamondhead demanded, as he shot off razor-sharp shards of crystalline glass that sliced the Sludge's arm in half, breaking his grip on Joel.

"A Petrosapien?!" exclaimed the Sludge, as he took a close look at Diamondhead. "What are you doing here?"

"Uh, I'm a friend of the groom," Diamondhead stammered.

"Then you're no friend of mine!" the Sludge raged, as he extended his regenerated limb toward his shimmering opponent.

Diamondhead dived out of the way and shot off a series of extremely pointy glass spears that passed harmlessly through the Sludge!

The two huge aliens then clashed in fierce battle, as the others in the room ducked for cover. As the giants grappled, they tumbled through the banquet-hall wall into the hotel's steam room.

In the thick mist of steam that rose from the sauna's rock pile, Diamondhead could not see the Sludge. Finally, however, he spotted a figure in the far corner.

"Gotcha!" he cried as he lurched forward. But it wasn't the Sludge he had spotted.

"*AAAAAH!!!*" shrieked the woman with the mud-packed face and cucumber-covered eyes, who Diamondhead had mistaken for the alien enemy.

"Uh, sorry, lady," an embarrassed Diamondhead apologized. "I thought you were a butt-ugly alien."

"Hmmph!" huffed the woman, as she stomped out of the destroyed room.

As she left, the Sludge emerged from a puddle on the sauna floor and grabbed Diamondhead from behind. Together, they tumbled through yet another wall – this time into the hotel's indoor swimming pool!

Diamondhead and the Sludge struggled desperately beneath the surface of the water, but the chlorine in the pool began taking its toll on the Sludge, causing him to relinquish his grip on Diamondhead.

As the Sludge dissipated, it escaped through the drain, leaving only a darkened, polluted trail behind. Diamondhead then made his way toward the side, as Gwen and Grandpa Max arrived.

"Yuck!" Diamondhead groaned, as he climbed out of the foul water and shook the mud off himself.

"It was a dirty job, but someone had to do it," Grandpa Max quipped.

"Unfortunately," Gwen predicted, as she peered into the bottom of the pool, "I don't think we've seen the last of the Sludge."

CHAPTER 4:
A Wedding to Remember

The time for the wedding was quickly approaching.

“You look like your underwear is too tight,” Gwen joked, as she entered the Rustbucket where Ben was awkwardly attempting to the follow the moves prescribed by a Waltz instructional video.

“Whoa!” a startled Ben said, while tripping over his own feet and falling down. Gwen was thoroughly enjoying the show.

“Are you sure you don’t want some one-to-one dance lessons?” she asked, adding, “especially since you seem to have two left feet.”

“Very funny!” a red-faced Ben shot back, as he got up and dusted himself off. “Now, buzz off!”

“How many times have I saved your superhero butt from space aliens and monsters?” Gwen asked.

“I don’t know. Maybe a couple of times,” Ben haltingly admitted.

“That was a rhetorical question, and the correct answer is more times than you can count.” Gwen reminded him.

"So?"

"So, if you can trust me to help fight intergalactic warlords, you should be able to trust me to teach you to dance."

"You're probably just gonna trick me into looking like a doofus," Ben said.

"Like you need my help for that. Now, get over yourself and give me your hands," Gwen commanded.

Reluctantly, Ben reached out and placed his hands in Gwen's.

"The most important thing," Gwen instructed as they assumed dancing positions, "is don't step on her toes."

"Ugh! This is so gross!" Ben griped.

"Like I don't know that," Gwen replied, as she began to lead him in a waltz. An hour later they were still at it. And both of them were surprised at Ben's progress.

"One, two. One, two. Forward, back. Forward, back," Gwen repeated.

"Hey, I'm dancing!" Ben shouted with pride. "Thanks!"

"You're welcome. See, all it took was a little trust."

“Aw, that is so sweet,” beamed Grandpa Max, who suddenly appeared in the doorway.

“Hey, get away from me!” a mortified Ben shouted to Gwen, while pushing her away. “I give up,” Gwen sighed. “I’m going for a walk.”

Gwen exited the Rustbucket and headed for the hotel lake, where she found Camille, alone and crying under the moonlight.

“What’s wrong?” Gwen asked.

“The wedding,” Camille sobbed, “I have to call it off.”

“Why?” Gwen responded with dismay. “Is it because of your ex-boyfriend?”

“No,” Camille answered. “I love Joel and only Joel. I want to spend my life with him.”

“So, why would you want to call off the wedding?”

“Because everyone’s against it. Earthlings and Sludges, both sides have told us that what we’re doing is wrong. We’re only creating more friction as the wedding nears. Maybe we’re not meant to be together.”

“Your parents seem supportive,” Gwen pointed out.

“Only in public,” Camille wept. “Your Grandpa Max is

the only one who's given us any real encouragement."

"Hey, there's me. Even my dweeby cousin Ben is for the wedding – he's just not too crazy about being in it. But that has nothing to do with you two being from different worlds. And, believe me, Lucy is *sooo* looking forward to being your flower girl. She doesn't care about any Earth-Sludge feud.

"In fact," Gwen continued, "kids like us depend on grown-ups like you and Joel to stand up and show us that ancient prejudices and hatreds can be overcome – with love. So, to me, the only real question is, 'Do you and Joel really love each other?'"

"Yes," Camille replied, "more than anything in the world."

"Then," Gwen pressed, "if, after searching your heart, you know your love to be true – and his love to be true – shouldn't that be enough? Shouldn't you both just trust your hearts? Why do you care what other people think?"

"You're right," Camille sniffed. "How'd you get to be so wise?"

"I don't know," Gwen smiled, "but thanks for noticing."

The next day, the sun shone brightly over the hotel

gazebo when Joel, handsome in his tuxedo, and Camille, beautiful in her bridal dress and veil, stood before a small gathering as the justice of the peace began the wedding service.

"Dearly beloved, we are gathered here to witness the union between Joel and Camille," he began as Ben, standing to the side, nervously clasped the pillow that held the couple's rings.

"This young couple," the justice of the peace continued, "reminds us all that true love really does conquer all. If anyone has a reason why these two should not wed, let them speak now or forever hold their..."

"Hold this!" shouted a voice from the gathering as – *SPLAT!* – the justice of the peace was drenched in a huge wad of mushy purple goo hurled from the assembly.

The shocked crowd gasped as they turned and saw that the thrower was none other than Mr. Mann,

Camille's father! What's more, his left arm had transformed into an amorphous violet ooze that dripped disgustingly from his shoulder.

"This wedding is over!" Mr. Mann declared, as an usher transformed into a Sludge and hurled purple muck at Big Gordon and Betty Jean, knocking them out of their chairs!

As the rest of the congregation ran for cover, Gwen, Ben, Grandpa Max, Big Gordon, and Betty Jean protectively surrounded Camille and Joel.

"This wedding – and every human here – is about to be cancelled!" Mr. Mann, flanked by Mrs. Mann and a Sludge enforcer, declared.

"Mom! Dad! What are you doing?!" Camille gasped.

"Sludges and Earthlings," her father insisted, "are not meant to live together!"

"And, especially, if the Sludge is our daughter!" her mother agreed.

"I don't get it," Ben said, "I thought they were the nice, easygoing ones."

"Things aren't always what they seem," Gwen offered. "They were behind the dirty tricks all along – even secretly goading Camille's ex-boyfriend into disrupting yesterday's luncheon. By exploiting the jealousy and prejudice of others, they threw suspicion off themselves."

"You're a smart girl – for an Earthling," Mr. Mann conceded, "but your brains won't save this marriage! There will be no wedding and no peace between the Plumbers and the Sludges! Never!"

With that, Mr. Mann thrust his slushy limb forward, grabbing Joel and lifting him high into the air.

"But – I – thought – you – liked – me!" Joel gurgled, as Mr. Mann's grip solidified and grew tighter around his throat.

With a shrug of his still-human shoulders, Mr. Mann matter-of-factly shouted back, "I lied!"

"*NO!!!*" Camille screamed, as she lunged toward her father.

"This is for your own good!"

Mrs. Mann insisted, as she changed into a Sludge, the transformation knocking her daughter backward toward the gazebo.

"That does it!" Ben raged, as he pounded his Omnitrix and became…HEATBLAST!

Camille watched in horror as the fiery alien hero faced off against the now-totally Sludgy Manns and their alien enforcer. As Heatblast charged toward them, his flames caused a mega-methane gas explosion that freed Joel, while also causing the would-be groom to fall about twenty feet onto the hotel lawn.

While the adults ran over to check on the unconscious Joel, Heatblast and Gwen faced off against the trio of Sludges, whose Swiss-cheese-like bodies were quickly reformulating!

Heatblast blasted them, but his flames passed harmlessly through their bodies! Realizing her cousin was in need of some magical help, Gwen raised her hands and uttered the spell *Sinew Invisibus!*

Rows of tables and chairs behind her transformed into mystical projectiles that darted toward the Sludges! But they, too, had no effect.

As Heatblast and Gwen fought the Sludges, Joel awakened to find Camille holding him in her arms.

"Are you okay?" she gently asked. He nodded, "Yes."

"Good," she replied with a smile, "cause no one's ruining my wedding day!" Camille then transformed into her Sludge self and joined Heatblast and Gwen in the battle against her parents and their Sludge enforcer.

"Isn't she beautiful?" Joel asked with pride, as he watched his fiancée fight for their love.

"Yes, she is," Big Gordon admitted.

Finally, after several minutes of non-stop brawling, Camille shouted out to Heatblast, "If you can go supernova, you'll evaporate the moisture inside them and they'll turn to stone!"

"Sounds good to me," Heatblast replied, "but you'd

better stand back." Heatblast then summoned all of his fiery energy to create a heat wave that quickly evaporated the moisture inside the Sludge bodies of Mr. and Mrs. Mann and their enforcer. And, just as Camille had said, they became alien masonry.

"Will they stay that way?" Gwen asked.

"No," Camille answered. "Once it rains – or the hotel sprinkler system kicks in – they'll become Sludges again."

"But, by that time, we'll be married," Joel interjected, as he kissed his soon-to-be-wife on the cheek.

And married they got – in a beautiful ceremony that was the start of a wonderful life together.

Joel's parents quickly put aside their old fears and accepted the union – and, eventually, Camille's parents did, too.

And everyone lived happily ever after.